jl Couture, S

W9-AVQ-005

The Biggest Horse I Ever Did See

BY SUSAN ARKIN COUTURE

ILLUSTRATED BY CLAIRE EWART

A LAURA GERINGER BOOK
AN IMPRINT OF HARPERCOLLINSPUBLISHERS

The Biggest Horse I Ever Did See

Copyright © 1997 by Susan Birkenhead, professionally known as Susan Arkin Couture.

Illustrations copyright © 1997 by Claire Ewart

Library of Congress Cataloging-in-Publication Data

Couture, Susan Arkin

  The biggest horse I ever did see / by Susan Arkin Couture ; illustrated by Claire Ewart.

    p.   cm.

  "A Laura Geringer book."

  Summary: A child yearningly watches a horse gallop over the mountain and imagines the part this animal might play in his future.

  ISBN 0-06-023467-9. — ISBN 0-06-023468-7 (lib. bdg.)

  [1. Horses—Fiction. 2. Imagination—Fiction. 3. Stories in rhyme.] I. Ewart, Claire, ill.
II. Title.

PZ8.3.C8335Bi 1997   95-23470

[Fic]—dc20   CIP
                                                            AC

Typography by Christine Kettner

1 2 3 4 5 6 7 8 9 10

❖

First Edition

For Peter, David, Richard, and Alison
—S. A. C.

For my father, John A. Ewart,
who taught me to persevere
—C. E.

The biggest horse I ever did see
Was galloping over the mountain
Galloping over the mountain in the morning.
He had stockings long and white
And he was such a splendid sight
Galloping over the mountain in the morning.

Another horse was by his side
Galloping over the mountain
Galloping over the mountain in the morning.

How I wished that I could ride
Upon their backs so strong and wide
Galloping over the mountain in the morning.

Then one day a team appeared
Galloping over the highway
Galloping over the highway in the morning.

Eight great horses thundering past
Pulling a wagon very fast
Galloping over the highway in the morning.

Two by two the horses came

Galloping over the highway

Galloping over the highway in the morning.

Since that day it's been my dream

To sit up there and drive that team
Galloping over the highway in the morning.

If I drove that splendid team
Galloping over the highway
Galloping over the highway in the morning,

When I got them home, I know,

I'd turn them loose so they could go

Galloping over the mountain in the morning

Galloping over the mountain in the morning

Galloping over the mountain in the morning.